To Jefrey —
Enjoy the Fair!
David Montgomery

MARCELO
VITTR

1904

Published by Van Gogh's Ear.
Cover, characters and compilation copyright © 2004
Marcelo Vital and David Montgomery. All rights reserved.
With exception of artwork used for review purposes, no portion of this
publication may be reproduced by any means without the expressed
written permission of the copyright holder.
www.1904ishere.com
ISBN 0-9754431-0-0
First edition: May 2004
PRINTED IN THE USA

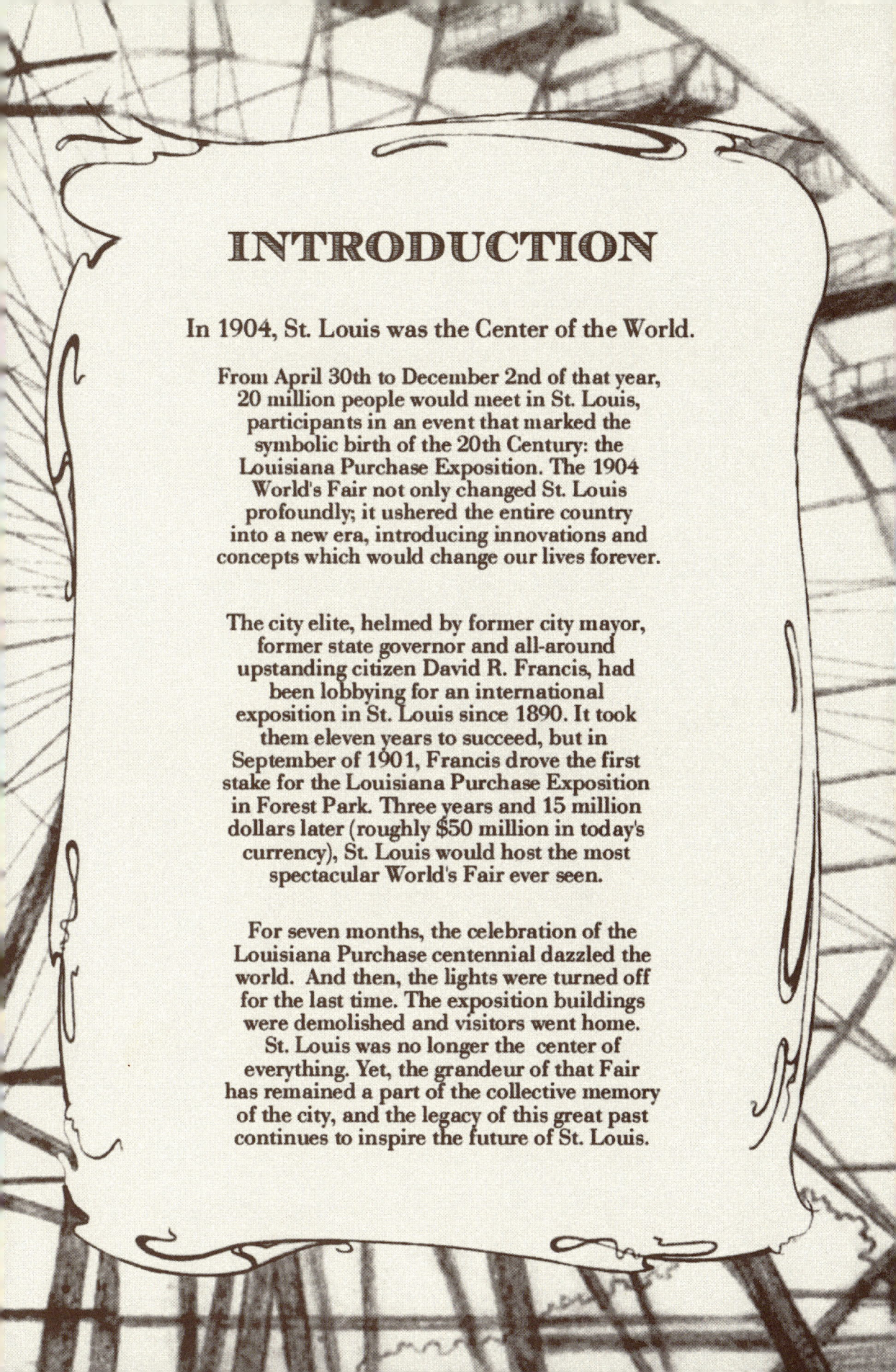

INTRODUCTION

In 1904, St. Louis was the Center of the World.

From April 30th to December 2nd of that year, 20 million people would meet in St. Louis, participants in an event that marked the symbolic birth of the 20th Century: the Louisiana Purchase Exposition. The 1904 World's Fair not only changed St. Louis profoundly; it ushered the entire country into a new era, introducing innovations and concepts which would change our lives forever.

The city elite, helmed by former city mayor, former state governor and all-around upstanding citizen David R. Francis, had been lobbying for an international exposition in St. Louis since 1890. It took them eleven years to succeed, but in September of 1901, Francis drove the first stake for the Louisiana Purchase Exposition in Forest Park. Three years and 15 million dollars later (roughly $50 million in today's currency), St. Louis would host the most spectacular World's Fair ever seen.

For seven months, the celebration of the Louisiana Purchase centennial dazzled the world. And then, the lights were turned off for the last time. The exposition buildings were demolished and visitors went home. St. Louis was no longer the center of everything. Yet, the grandeur of that Fair has remained a part of the collective memory of the city, and the legacy of this great past continues to inspire the future of St. Louis.

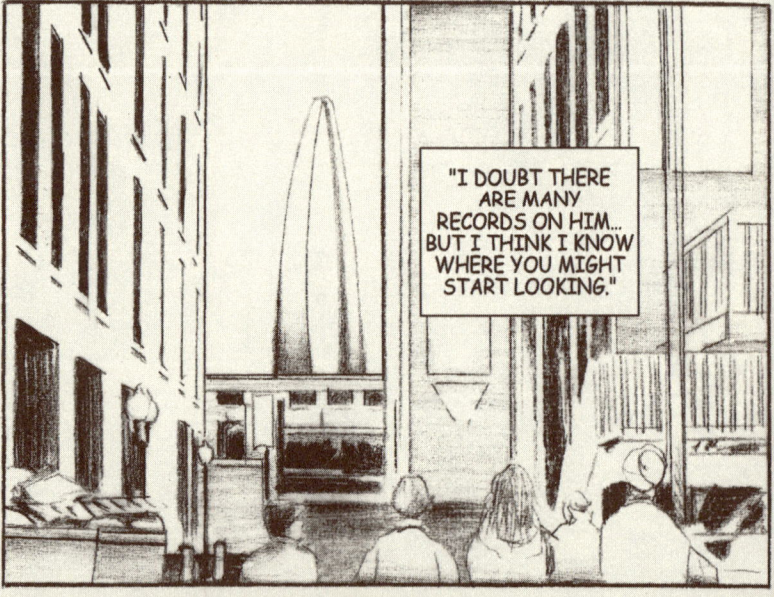

"GO TO YOUR NONNA'S HOUSE ON THE HILL...

...AND CHECK IN HER BASEMENT. YOU'LL FIND ALL THE THINGS YOUR GRANDPA STORED BEFORE HE DIED.

I'M SURE YOUR GRANDMA WON'T MIND IF YOU LOOK AROUND.

THERE'RE ALL KINDS OF KNICKKNACKS IN THERE - FAMILY PORTRAITS, ANCIENT RECIPE BOOKS, PICTURES OF OLD RELATIVES, YOU NAME IT. SOME OF IT IS MORE THAN A HUNDRED YEARS OLD, FROM WAY BACK WHEN OUR FAMILY FIRST ARRIVED FROM ITALY.

WHO KNOWS WHAT YOU MIGHT FIND IN THERE.

YOU MIGHT EVEN GET LUCKY AND FIND SOMETHING VALUABLE!

ST. LOUIS PHOTOSTAT CO., LOUISIANA PURCHASE EXPOSITION

Nico d'Chiara 1904

MAYBE YOU WON'T FIND ANYTHING FOR YOUR PAPER...

May 2, 1904

Meet me in St. Louis, Louie
Meet me at the Fair
Don't tell me
the lights are shining
Any place but there

If the crowds on opening day were any indication of what's to come, it's going to be grand.

...BUT IT'S AT LEAST WORTH A TRY, DON'T YOU THINK?"

I should have known better, of course. Everything had been just a bit too good to be true.

In all fairness, how fortunate can one fellow expect to be? First, I'm alive for the one-hundredth anniversary of the Louisiana Purchase, an event second only to the Declaration of Independence.

Second, I just happen to live in the city chosen to host the Fair that celebrates the centennial. (And who cares if the party is a year late? Something this amazing is well worth the wait!)

And to top it all off, I get a job with the Louisiana Purchase Exposition Company, which means I see the Fair for free everyday.

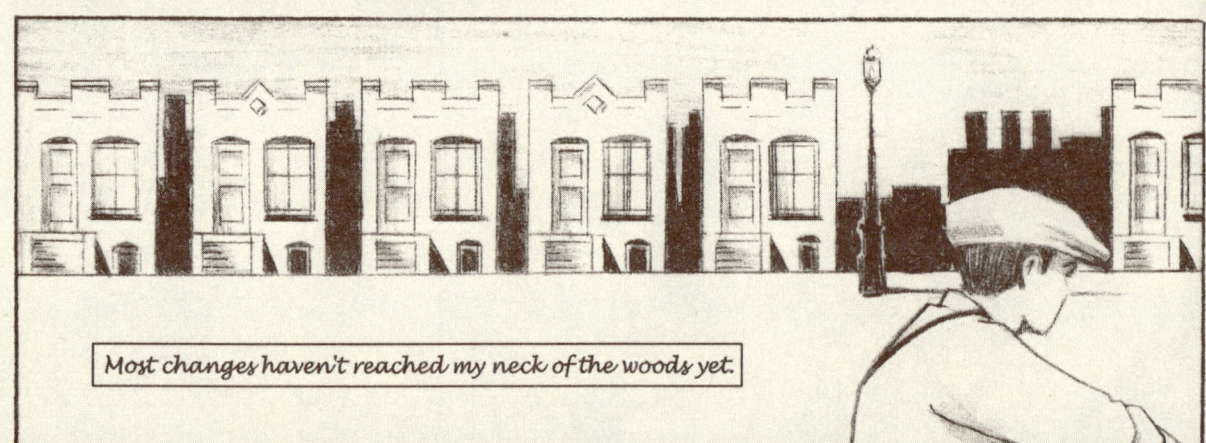

The Palace of Electricity!

Looking back, it sounded like a good idea. The palace is a highlight of the Fair, and we hadn't spent much time inside yet.

As you enter the Palace, you're surrounded by the whirring, snapping and flashing of strange machines and ingenious contraptions that demonstrate the power of electricity and all its wonders -- from the latest innovations in incandescent light bulbs to the mysterious properties of the x-ray.

All courtesy, of course, of one very distinguished gentleman...

CLAIRE, LOOK! THOMAS EDISON!!

Mr. Edison had come to the Fair to supervise the installation of the electric lights, and we were lucky enough to catch him doing a demonstration!

I stood there for a minute, admiring that great man behind all those levers and cables bustling with electricity, all that power at his fingertips.

Watching him, the future looked so full of possibilities...

I told Claire I wanted to use a telephone to call cousin Primo up in New York. He'd never believe I saw the Wizard of Menlo Park in the flesh!

I'LL MEET YOU BACK HERE IN TEN MINUTES.

SEE YOU THEN!

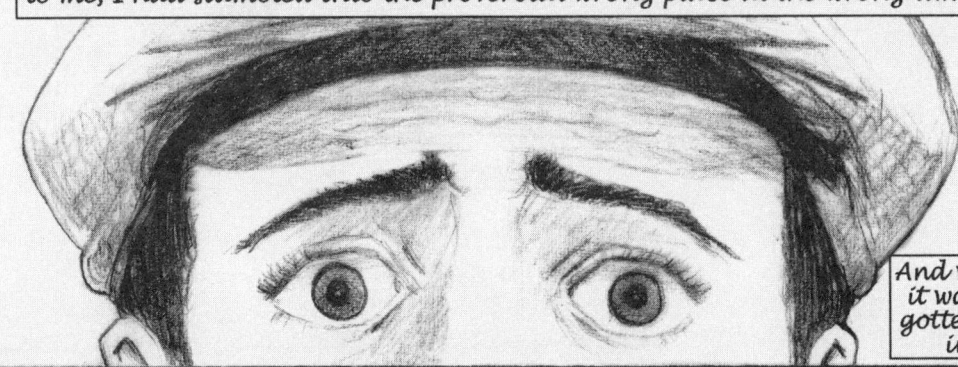

1904

STORY MARCELO VITAL
ART DAVID MONTGOMERY

> The World's Fair Bulletin says that there's something at the Exposition for everyone to enjoy, no matter what their fancy.

> With the world laid out before you, the options are endless and not always what you'd expect.

> At the 1904 World's Fair there's always a surprise just around the corner.

Chapter Two: Down the Pike

You just never know what awaits you or whom you might run into.

The one thing you won't find at the Louisiana Purchase Exposition though, is a dull moment.

In the Palace of Transportation, for instance, you can see everything from the first steam engine to the most modern automobile.

Just blocks away is the walled city of Jerusalem, a labyrinth of narrow passages teeming with street vendors and peculiar sights.

More peaceful an endeavor is a trip to the Japanese Garden where daintily clad geishas serve tea to visitors resting from the bustle of the Fair.

If you're lucky, you might even catch a glimpse of genuine Sioux chiefs and warriors dressed for their dance ceremony.

All this without ever leaving the fairgrounds.

> Now, that same wheel is in our own Forest Park, all 260 feet and 4,000 tons of it, with 36 cars taking 60 fairgoers each to new heights, new sights and new sensations. That's more than 2,000 people! And the ones not brave enough to go up in it still enjoy watching it from the ground, mesmerized as mr. Ferris' invention spins like one mighty bicycle wheel.

HOW MAJESTIC! THAT EIFFEL TOWER FROM THE PARIS EXPOSITION SURELY HAS NOTHING ON OUR WHEEL. BESIDES, WHAT FUN IS GOING UP AND DOWN WHEN YOU CAN GO ROUND AND ROUND?

I HOPE THEY'LL KEEP IT HERE FOREVER!

I wished I could share in Claire's enthusiasm, but I was still shaken by my run-in with those fellas.

I MUST ADMIT I'M A BIT SCARED...

I just couldn't keep it all to myself any longer. I had to tell somebody what happened, even if it sounded crazy.

...OH MY, IT'S MOVING!

I had to tell Claire the truth.

THIS IS SO MUCH FUN, NICO! YOU CAN SEE HOW LARGE THE FAIR REALLY IS FROM UP HERE. LOOK, ALL THE PEOPLE LOOK LIKE TINY ANTS DOWN THERE.
JERUSALEM
IT'S SO ROMANTIC, TOO...
CLAIRE, I...I'VE GOT SOMETHING I NEED TO TELL YOU.
YES, NICO. WHAT IS IT?
I THINK SOMEBODY IS TRYING TO KILL ME.
HA! HA! HA! OH, NICO, YOU ALMOST HAD ME WITH THAT ONE!
YOUR EXCUSES ARE USUALLY INCREDIBLE, BUT THIS TAKES THE CAKE!
I'M SERIOUS, CLAIRE!
THESE GUYS... I THINK THEY WERE GANGSTERS -- FROM CHICAGO!
WHAT? FOR GOODNESS SAKES, NICO, WHAT ARE YOU TALKING ABOUT? IF THIS IS ANOTHER ONE OF YOUR PRANKS...
I WISH IT WERE, CLAIRE. I REALLY DO.
THIS IS HOW IT HAPPENED...

Two revolutions and some revelations later...
HMM, THAT'S QUITE A STORY... DID YOU TELL THE POLICE?
NO, NOT YET... I WANTED TO TELL YOU FIRST TO MAKE SURE I'M NOT LOSING MY MIND.
FRANKLY, NICO... IT SOUNDS SORT OF...
OUTLANDISH?
WELL, IT'S JUST THAT, FOR ALL WE KNOW, THIS COULD'VE JUST BEEN A SIMPLE MISUNDERSTANDING. I MEAN, A REALLY, REALLY TERRIBLE ONE!
BUT THERE'S NO WAY TO BE SURE, RIGHT?
WHAT I'M TRYING TO SAY IS, YOU MAY BE WORRYING ABOUT SOMETHING THAT... THAT WASN'T WHAT YOU THOUGHT IT WAS.
SO YOU DON'T BELIEVE ME?
NO, I DO...I JUST DON'T THINK YOU SHOULD TAKE IT SO SERIOUSLY. YOU PROBABLY WON'T EVER SEE THOSE HOODLUMS AGAIN. AND IF YOU DO, WE'LL CALL THE POLICE RIGHT AWAY.
NOW LET'S TRY TO FORGET ALL ABOUT THIS AND ENJOY THE REST OF THE FAIR LIKE WE HAD PLANNED, ALL RIGHT?

Being so high up can really change your perspective. It didn't take much arm-twisting to follow Claire's advice.

LISTEN, JACK... I'M SURE WE'LL RUN INTO HIM AGAIN SOONER OR LATER. NOW QUIT YOUR WHINING ABOUT THIS GARZONNE...

She was right after all. What were the chances of running into those fellas again in a place this size, right?

WHAT IF HE DECIDES TO SPILL THE BEANS?

WHAT BEANS? HE'S GOT NO BEANS TO SPILL!

HOW CAN YOU BE SO SURE? YOU DON'T KNOW HOW MUCH HE HEARD...

IT DON'T MATTER WHAT HE HEARD! IT'S TOO LATE FOR HIM TO DO ANYTHING. 'SIDES, WHO'D BELIEVE HIM ANYWAY?

"LISTEN, THIS JOB IS THE BIG TIME. WE AIN'T GOT TIME TO WORRY ABOUT SOME LITTLE KID.

NOW, WHY DID YOU BRING US UP HERE?"

"RECONNAISSANCE, MORON. FROM UP HERE WE'LL BE ABLE TO SCOPE OUT THE FAIRGROUNDS BETTER. NOW GIMME THE MAP."

I AIN'T GOT THE DARN MAP! I GAVE IT TO YOU.

NO, NO YOU DIDN'T! I TOLD YOU TO KEEP IT, CRETINO. I REMEMBER PERFECTLY...

HEY, FELLAS, KEEP IT DOWN, WILL YA? I'M TRYING TO 'PRECIATE THE VIEW.

When troubles get you down, there's a special place at the World's Fair that will bring your spirits right back up.

We call it the Pike!

It's a mile-long stretch unlike any on Earth, full of unfamiliar sights, sounds and scents, alive with exotic music, entertaining concessions and thrilling rides. The Pike is also the melting pot of the Fair. All creeds and customs are found there.

You can visit Ancient Rome, ride a burro to see the cliff dwellers, or go deep-sea diving; you can relive the Galveston Flood, witness a Naval Battle and go down a Magic Whirlpool; you can go from New York to the North Pole, visit the bazaars of Istanbul and the Streets of Seville, and still have time to see Constantinople and the Irish Village.

Last Sunday at Mass, Father Cesare said that if it was a mile longer, the Pike would lead straight to hell.

I figure his visit to the Pike must've been a bad one.

Me, I think it leads straight to a grand time.

Especially if you have someone to go down the Pike with you.

'ep, at the Pike everything is possible.

First we went through Creation, where the seven days of Genesis are squeezed into a ten-minute boat ride.

Then, we caught the Wild West show in Old St. Louis (where else could you get Geronimo and Will Rogers on the same bill?)

Our next stop was a real crowd-pleaser and Claire's favorite place on the Pike: the Baby Incubators. There, visitors watch how nurses care for the tiny mites of humanity using the most modern machines available to medicine.

After that, it was on to Fair Japan. Once we got past the fearsome-looking dragons, we were impressed by the country's unique progress and traditions.

Of course, there's always a gay crowd at Cabaret Braun in Paris, the haunt of bohemians, café types and racy dancing girls.

Education may take center stage at the Palaces in the Main Picture, but at the Pike, it's fun and excitement that are in the spotlight.

The visit to the Pike made me forget all about the fix I'd gotten myself into earlier.
— ST. LOUIS — PHOTOSTAT CO.
I wish those moments could last forever... even with all the innovations around here, they still haven't invented a machine to do that. But there are close alternatives.
STANT CTURE- AKING CHINE 5¢
WO FA SOU 5
ANKFURTERS
RED HOTS!! RED HOTS!!
GET YOUR RED HOTS HERE!
After an afternoon of frolicking, we got mighty hungry, too. As you might expect, even the food around here is novel.
NICO...
CLAIRE, WHAT'S WRONG? YOU LOOK SO PALE!
I'M NOT FEELING VERY...
CLAIRE!!

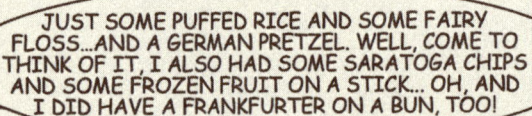

Luckily the emergency hospital on Model Street is just a stone's throw away from the Pike.

DR. LAIDLEY! DR. LAIDLEY! PLEASE HELP!! SOMETHING'S WRONG WITH CLAIRE!

WELL, LET'S SEE HERE! HMM. PULSE IS FINE, TEMPERATURE'S NORMAL...

TELL ME, YOUNG LADY, WHAT DID YOU HAVE TO EAT TODAY?

NOTHING REALLY, DOCTOR...

JUST SOME PUFFED RICE AND SOME FAIRY FLOSS... AND A GERMAN PRETZEL. WELL, COME TO THINK OF IT, I ALSO HAD SOME SARATOGA CHIPS AND SOME FROZEN FRUIT ON A STICK... OH, AND I DID HAVE A FRANKFURTER ON A BUN, TOO!

MY WORD! NO WONDER YOU'RE NOT FEELING WELL, MY DEAR. THOSE SO-CALLED "FAST FOODS" FROM THE PIKE ARE AN INVITATION TO DYSPEPSIA.

HERE. THIS NEW HYDRATING TONIC SHALL COUNTERACT YOUR INDIGESTION SYMPTOMS AND BRING YOU NEW SPIRITS.

BURP

WHY, THANK YOU VERY MUCH, DR. LAIDLEY! THAT WAS QUITE WHAT I NEEDED.

NOW I FEEL EQUAL TO ANYTHING!

VERY GOOD! NOW GO TAKE IN SOME FRESH AIR, AND AVOID FIERCE RIDES -- NO "SHOOTING THE CHUTES" OR GOING "OVER AND UNDER THE SEA" FOR YOU, YOU HEAR? AND, IF YOU WILL...

"...SLOW DOWN ON THE FAST-FOODS OUT THERE!"

Slowing down were the doctor's orders, and they were fine by me - I sure needed some rest after all that had happened that day.

We were close to Commonwealth Avenue, and I thought a visit to the Terrace of States would be a mild enough activity for the afternoon. It'd be best for Claire to stay away from the Main Picture of the Fair for a while.

Forty-three of the 45 States sent delegations to the World's Fair, and forty have buildings where folks can rest, admire art exhibits and enjoy some genuine homespun hospitality. Each State building is nicer than the next, and they're quite a sight too, all in the same neighborhood.

Good Missourians that we are, we decided to spend some time in our own State Building.

Of course Missouri has the largest of the state buildings, and the finest, too!

It even has a cooling system that keeps visitors fresh on the hottest of days. Small wonder it's such a popular destination!

But that afternoon, I didn't even need the cooling system to get chilled to the bone.

It was him! One of those thugs who tried to rough me up at the Palace of Electricity!

With all the million places to go around here, why did he have to be at the Missouri Building?

He saw me, I'm sure, but didn't care to stop.

Seemed to be in a great hurry for some reason.

I watched him take off with his buddies in one of those noisy new motor cars, disappearing in a trail of dust.

But what in blazes were they doing there?

Somehow I doubted that character had just come in to see the governor's portrait...

Soon enough I'd understand the purpose of his visit.

FIRE!!

The whole thing happened in a flash. All of a sudden, there was smoke everywhere, and folks were running amok.

It was a mad rush to get out, but everywhere we turned...

...another wall of fire blocked the way.

This was not what I wanted my last memory of the Fair to be.

The fire was already raging out of control and the smoke was thick as a wool blanket. The temperature was rising and I had the sinking feeling...
...things were about to get even hotter.
CHAPTER TWO
END

1904

STORY
MARCELO VITAL

ART
DAVID MONTGOMERY

At the Louisiana Purchase Exposition, it's hard be certain if what you're witnessing is real or make-believe. At times, what you see is so unbelievable that a body can't be blamed for thinking it must be another illusion.

Sometimes the sight is so frightful that you hope it is.

CHAPTER THREE

No Small Plans

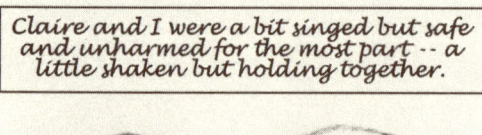

Alas, the fire at the Missouri Building was very real.

I should know... I was there.

By the time the firefighters got to the building, all they could do was save some paintings, some furniture and some mighty scared folks.

Thankfully, no one was hurt, but not even Hale's champion firefighters could save the building.

Most of the Missouri was a goner before you could say "Borax Bill and his Team of Twenty Mules."

Claire and I were a bit singed but safe and unharmed for the most part -- a little shaken but holding together.

In the middle of all that confusion and running around, there was only one thing on my mind though: What were those types who had chased me earlier doing at the Missouri Building right before the fire started? Coincidence? I found that hard to swallow. They left in an awful hurry.

When I asked a fireman about the cause of the blaze, he told me it was electric. I asked him if there was anything suspect about it.

ARSON? NAH... MORE LIKELY ACCIDENTAL. SURPRISING IT DOESN'T HAPPEN A LOT MORE OFTEN, REALLY, ALL THEM WOOD BUILDINGS 'ROUND HERE...

I decided not to tell him anything about the scary fellas. At the time, it didn't seem like a good idea to get myself mixed up with that fiery mess.

Besides, I was still hoping that my suspicions were wrong.

On the way home I told Claire what I was thinking. After all that happened that night, I think she was starting to believe me.

She wasn't entirely convinced, for sure, but I could tell she was getting a bit scared, too.

She told me I should talk to the Jefferson Guards in the morning just in case, for my peace of mind.

Lord knows I needed some.

NICO, IS THAT YOU?

MAMA SAID YES, NICO! SHE SAID I CAN GO TO THE FAIR WITH YOU AND RIDE A CAMEL!

THAT'S GREAT, MAX! BUT YOU'D BETTER GO TO SLEEP NOW -- DON'T WANNA WAKE UP MAMA.

WE'LL TALK MORE ABOUT THE FAIR TOMORROW, OK?

BUONA NOTTE.

Wish I could've had a good night, but the excitement of the fire plus all those thoughts and questions in my head didn't let me sleep a wink.

I was really wishing my suspicions were wrong, and that I was worrying for naught.

But what if I was right? What if there was no Fair left to take Massimo to?

NICO, WHAT'S WRONG WITH YOU? YOU DIDN'T SLEEP RIGHT?
I'M GONNA RIDE A CAMEL, I'M GONNA RIDE A CAMEL...
HUH?
OH, YEAH, MAMA, I DIDN'T SLEEP VERY WELL...
NO, THERE IS SOMETHING ELSE...
IS IT CHIARA?
NO, MAMA, IT'S NOTHING TO DO WITH CLAIRE. I'M JUST TIRED, THAT'S ALL.
DON'T WAIT FOR ME TONIGHT. I'M TAKING CLAIRE TO SEE THE LIGHTS AND FIREWORKS.
No point in telling Mama what happened. She'd just add it to her list of worries, and that's long enough as it is.
It's been tough since Papa died. With Massimo and baby Lucia and everything else... We get by, but it's pretty hard sledding.
No reason to put more weight on her shoulders.

The Palace of Education and Social Economy is a showcase for all the latest teaching methods from kindergarten to college. The exhibit has model schools from around the world with live action classrooms and students in them.

In the Palace you can also find an exhibit of the most modern crime-fighting techniques presented by real law officers of the Jefferson Guard.

Even if it sounded preposterous, I had to tell the police. As Claire said, they'd probably thank me for the tip.

HA! HA! HA!!

MOBSTERS??? FROM CHICAGO, YOU SAY?

HA! HA! HA!!

SETTING THE MISSOURI BUILDING ON FIRE, HUH??

HEE! HEE!!

NOW, THAT'S A NEW ONE...

LISTEN, SON, WE APPRECIATE YOUR CONCERN FOR THE FAIR...
...BUT WE'VE GOT PLENTY ON OUR HANDS TODAY AS IT IS, WITH THE HOLIDAY AND EVERYTHING.
BU...
DO YOU HAVE ANY IDEA HOW MANY PEOPLE ARE AT THE FAIR THIS WEEKEND, YOUNG MAN?
AND THIS WHOLE STORY OF YOURS IS A LITTLE FAR-FETCHED, DON'T YA THINK? ARE YOU TRYING TO COVER UP FOR SOME TROUBLE YOU GOT YOURSELF INTO?
NEVER MIND MY COLLEAGUE, SON. LISTEN, WE'LL KEEP AN EYE OUT, SPECIALLY FOR A FELLA WITH A, A... WHAT WAS IT AGAIN?
A SPUR FOR A HAND!
THAT'S RIGHT, A SPUR FOR A HAND!
TELL YOU WHAT. IF YOU SEE THEM FELLAS AGAIN, COME TELL US AND WE'LL BRING'EM IN FOR QUESTIONING.
NOW WHY DON'T YOU GO AND HAVE A LOOK AT OUR CRIMINOLOGY EXHIBIT. THAT SHOULD PUT YOUR MIND AT EASE.
DID YOU KNOW NOW WE'RE ABLE TO IDENTIFY CRIMINALS JUST BY THE PRINTS ON THEIR FINGERS?
BUT CHIEF, THIS GUY AIN'T GOT NO FINGERS... HAR!
ENOUGH, FRANK!
TRY AND STAY OUT OF TROUBLE, YOU HEAR, SON?
BLAM!

SO? HOW DID IT GO?
THEY DIDN'T BELIEVE ME.
WHY WOULD THEY, AFTER ALL?
...CAN BARELY BELIEVE IT MYSELF...
OH, NICO, I'M SO SORRY...
HERE, THIS SHOULD HELP LIFT YOUR SPIRITS!
I BROUGHT YOU A WORLD'S FAIR CORNUCOPIA!
I KNOW DOCTOR LAIDLEY TOLD US TO STAY AWAY FROM THE PIKE NOVELTIES, BUT... WHO CAN RESIST ICE CREAM IN A WAFFLE CONE?
MISSOURI
After a morning like that, I was glad to at least have Claire to cheer me up.

SO, WHAT AM I SUPPOSED TO DO NOW?

THERE'S NOTHING TO DO, NICO! YOU'VE DONE ALL YOU COULD. NOW YOU NEED TO TRY AND ENJOY THE REST OF OUR HOLIDAY.

BUT WHAT IF WE RUN INTO THEM...

IF YOU EVER LAY EYES ON THOSE HOODLUMS AGAIN, WE'LL GO STRAIGHT TO THE POLICE STATION AND TELL THE JEFFERSON GUARDS ABOUT IT. BUT UNTIL THAT HAPPENS, IF IT HAPPENS, IT'LL DO YOU NO GOOD TO FRET ABOUT IT ALL DAY LONG.

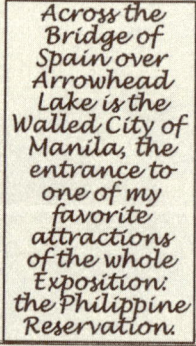

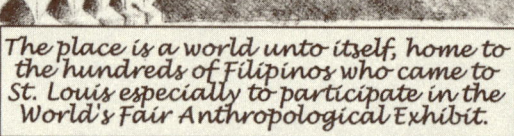

NOW, PERHAPS A TRIP AROUND THE WORLD WILL OCCUPY YOUR MIND IN A MORE PLEASANT WAY!

Lucky for us, the Fair makes traveling 'round the world as easy as crossing the street. They say you can see more in one day at the Fair than in months of traveling abroad. You can go from Europe to the Orient and back to the Americas in just a few yards' distance.

United Kingdom

Belgium

Brazil

Siam

The Exposition has brought the world to our doorstep.

Across the Bridge of Spain over Arrowhead Lake is the Walled City of Manila, the entrance to one of my favorite attractions of the whole Exposition: the Philippine Reservation.

The place is a world unto itself, home to the hundreds of Filipinos who came to St. Louis especially to participate in the World's Fair Anthropological Exhibit.

They lead their daily lives right here in front of us, so we get to see how they live, what they eat and how they dress. Some of their customs may seem downright odd to us...

NICO, LOOK!

SMOKE!!

...but the Fair just wouldn't be the same without them.

The reservation is like a little piece of the Philippines. I've learned that there are many kinds of Filipinos, all quite different from each other: Igorot, Negrito, Moro, Tagalog, Bagobo, Visayan... anywhere from dressed-up to not dressed at all -- much to Lady Managers' chagrin.

If it wasn't for the Fair, I'd never know these folks existed. But I got to learn their names, see theirs houses, play with their kids... I even made friends!

I care about them now 'cause I got to know them.

I may prefer my hot dogs coming from a concession at the Pike...

They are our guests, and we St. Louisians are notorious good hosts -- even if our tastes differ from those of our guests.

...but everyone feels bad just the same when a good barbecue goes awry.

IGOROT VILLAGE HEAD HUNTER OF THE PHILIPPINES

I had a one-track mind that afternoon, despite Claire's attempts to distract me. Everywhere I looked, trouble was all I could see.

But if I were to enjoy the rest of the day, I had to shake those worries from my mind. I had to find a way to convince myself that, wherever those ruffians were at that moment...

...they'd already forgotten about me.
SEE HIM ANYWHERE?
OF COURSE HE DON'T. DO YOU REALLY EXPECT TO SPOT THE KID FROM UP HERE, JACK?
WHY ARE YOU SO HOT AFTER THIS RUNT, ANYWAY?
DANNY, YOU IDIOTA, I TOLD YOU! HE SAW ME AT THE MISSOURI BUILDING -- AND I SAW HIM TALKING TO THE FIREMEN, TOO.
SO WHAT?
LISTEN, JACK. OUR JOB IS ALMOST FINITO, NO MATTER WHAT THIS KID DOES.
THE LITTLE PUKE MAY HAVE ESCAPED LAST NIGHT, BUT HE WON'T BE ESCAPING TONIGHT...
HEY, FELLAS! I THINK YOU MIGHT WANNA TAKE A PEEK AT THIS...

I CAN'T SEE ANYTHING!

WHERE ARE WE?

ALRIGHT, YOU CAN LOOK NOW.

OH, NICO! A GONDOLA!! JUST LIKE MY NONNO'S IN VENICE!!

WELL, I KNEW HOW BADLY YOU WANTED TO GO ON A GONDOLA RIDE, SINCE YOU MENTION YOUR GRANDPA EVERY TIME WE SEE A BOAT! SO I ASKED GIUSEPPE IF I COULD BORROW HIS FOR THE AFTERNOON AND I EVEN TALKED HIM INTO LETTING ME STEER IT.

NOW, PER FAVORE, SIT BACK AND ENJOY. FOR YOUR PLEASURE, I'LL REFRAIN FROM SINGING...

The Grand Basin is the heart of the Main Picture, pumping water down cascades and fountains and entrancing fairgoers from all around. You can see it no matter where you are, and it's never the same view twice. But the best view is from inside.

If you follow the full circuit of the Grand Basin and its Lagoons, you'll notice fascinating new angles of the architecture and landscape of the Fair. To one side, the Palaces of Mines and Metallurgy, Liberal Arts, Manufactures and Education. To the other, Machinery, Transportation, Varied Industries and Electricity.

The waterways are usually swarming with scores of launches and other types of boats. There's even parades with gaily-decorated boats gliding through the waters from time to time. On a boat, you'll see vistas like none available on terra firma.

It's an hour of enchantment, as Claire likes to say.

Panel 1:
- "IT'S ALL SOOO LOVELY... IT MAKES YOU WONDER, DOESN'T IT?"
- "WONDER WHAT?"

Panel 2:
- "WELL, YOU KNOW... JUST A HUNDRED YEARS AGO WE WERE JUST A TINY FUR TRADING POST AT THE EDGE OF THE LOUISIANA PURCHASE. AND LOOK AT OUR ST. LOUIS NOW! THE CENTER OF THE WORLD, A COSMOPOLITAN CITY HOSTING THE MOST SPECTACULAR WORLD'S FAIR EVER! NOT TO MENTION THE FIRST OLYMPIC GAMES IN AMERICA, TOO!"

Panel 3:
- "YEAH, WE'VE COME A LONG WAY SINCE THE LEWIS AND CLARK DAYS."
- "CAN YOU IMAGINE WHERE WE'LL BE IN HUNDRED YEARS?"

Panel 4:
- "HMM, BURIED?"
- "NO, SILLY, THAT'S NOT WHAT I MEANT... DO YOU THINK -- DO YOU THINK PEOPLE WILL REMEMBER THE FAIR THEN?"

Panel 5:
- "IN A HUNDRED YEARS? WHY, CLAIRE, I SHOULD HOPE SO!"

Panel 6:
- "HOW COULD ANYONE FORGET SOMETHING LIKE THIS?"

THAT WAS JUST WONDERFUL, NICO, THANKS!
I'M OFF NOW TO MEET LOTTIE AT THE PALACE OF MANUFACTURES. I PROMISED I'D ACCOMPANY HER ON A VISIT TO THE FRENCH LACE EXHIBIT. ARE YOU SURE YOU DON'T WANT TO COME ALONG?
YEAH, VERY SURE. I THINK I CAN STILL CATCH THE MINING GULCH BEFORE IT CLOSES FOR THE DAY.
VERY WELL THEN. WHERE SHOULD WE MEET TO WATCH THE ILLUMINATIONS AND THE FIREWORKS TONIGHT? IT MUST BE SOMEPLACE WITH AN EXCELLENT VIEW OF THE PALACE OF ELECTRICITY, IF YOU PLEASE!
WHAT ABOUT THE DANIEL BOONE BRIDGE? IT'S CLOSE TO MANUFACTURES AND IT'LL GIVE US A GOOD VIEW.
PERFECT! I'LL WAIT FOR YOU THERE BY TWILIGHT. DON'T BE LATE!
MIA CARA, I WOULDN'T MISS IT EVEN IF ALL THE MOBSTERS IN SICILY WERE AFTER ME!
HA HA! GOOD TO SEE YOU GOT YOUR GOOD SPIRITS BACK. SEE YOU AT THE GRAND FINALE!

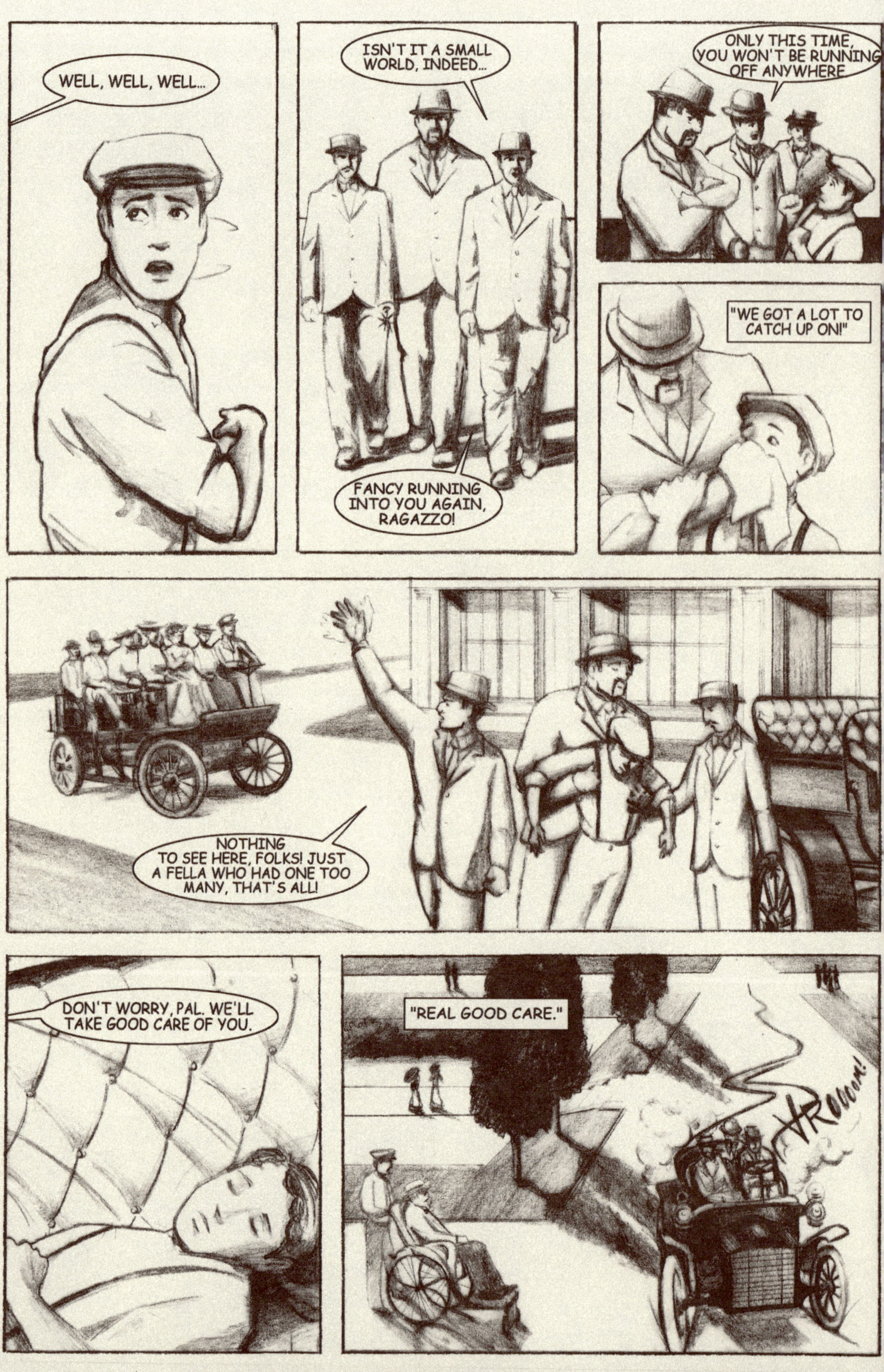
WELL, WELL, WELL...
ISN'T IT A SMALL WORLD, INDEED...
FANCY RUNNING INTO YOU AGAIN, RAGAZZO!
ONLY THIS TIME, YOU WON'T BE RUNNING OFF ANYWHERE
"WE GOT A LOT TO CATCH UP ON!"
NOTHING TO SEE HERE, FOLKS! JUST A FELLA WHO HAD ONE TOO MANY, THAT'S ALL!
DON'T WORRY, PAL. WE'LL TAKE GOOD CARE OF YOU.
"REAL GOOD CARE."
VROOOOM!

Was this really happening? Or was I dreaming? I couldn't really tell. If it was a dream, it was an awful bad one.

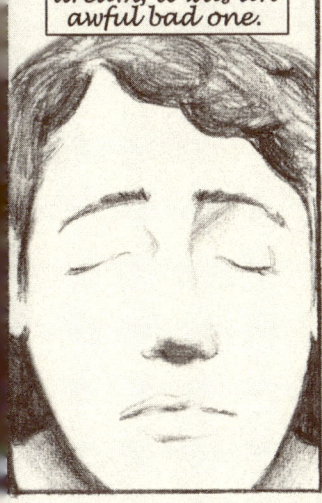

Everything was blurry and the world seemed out of focus. I could tell I was moving, but I didn't know where.

I was trying really hard to stay awake, or at least I dreamt I was trying. Then, right in the middle of it all, an image appeared in front of me.

It was Massimo, my poor little brother. I was thinking of him, of how much I wanted to bring him to the Fair.

Now, who was going to take him for a camel ride?

That was my last thought before everything... turned...

... dark.

C'MON, MOVE IT! HE'S WAKING UP!
TRAINED ANIMAL CIRCUS
CARL HAGENBECK'S
THUNK
OUCH!
WHERE AM...
YOU!!
OH, LOOK WHO'S AWAKE! WE WERE AFRAID YOU'D BE ALL TUCKERED OUT FOR THE PARTY!
WE FIGURED YOU BEING SUCH A CURIOUS CAT, WHAT BETTER PLACE TO BRING YOU THAN TO THE ANIMAL PARADISE?
HELP!!
YOU CAN YELL 'TIL YOU'RE BLUE IN THE FACE, KID. IT'S ALMOST CANDLE-LIGHTING AND HAGENBECK'S IS CLOSED FOR THE DAY. EVERYBODY'S GONE.
FINALLY, IT'S JUST YOU...
...AND US.

THIS MUST BE A MISUNDERSTANDING! I'M JUST A DELIVERY BOY! I...
WHAT YOU ARE IS A NOSY KID WHO'S BEEN AROUND A LITTLE TOO MUCH. I SAW YOU LAST NIGHT, TALKING TO THE FIREMAN.
THE FIRE IN THE MISSOURI BUILDING! YOU DID DO IT!!
AND THE EXPLOSION IN THE INSIDE INN HOTEL, THE FIRE AT THE HOUSE OF HOO HOO, THE FAIR-BOUND TRAIN WRECK IN WARRENS-BURG, THE ELEPHANT RAGE IN THE FILIPINO CAMP... AND SOME OTHER LITTLE "ACCIDENTS."
SO IT'S TRUE... YOU REALLY ARE TRYING TO SPOIL THE FAIR!
SPOIL? NO, NOT JUST SPOIL. WE WANNA EXFLUNCTICATE THE PLACE! SEND IT ALL TO HELL!
IT'LL JUST BE ANOTHER ACCIDENT, OF COURSE... THE BIGGEST OF THEM ALL.
WHAT? WHAT ARE YOU SAYING?
LET'S JUST SAY THAT TONIGHT, WHEN EVERYONE GATHERS 'ROUND TO SEE THE HOLIDAY LIGHTS AND PYRO-TECHNICS, THEY'LL GET MORE FIRE-WORKS THAN THEY BARGAINED FOR.
TELL ME, KID... WHAT DO YOU GET WHEN YOU SURROUND TWO HUNDRED THOUSAND PEOPLE WITH TONS OF FLAMMABLE MATERIALS, ALL LACED WITH THIRTY THOUSAND KILOWATTS OF... ELECTRICITY!!
BBZZZZZ!!
YOU SEE, THERE'LL BE A LITTLE ACCIDENT TONIGHT AT THE GREAT ELECTRIC SWITCHBOARD, A POWER SURGE THAT WILL CAUSE AN ALMIGHTY SHORT-CIRCUIT ALL THROUGHOUT THESE LIGHT-BULBIFIED FAIRGROUNDS, BURNING EVERY TRANSFORMER IN EVERY PALACE AND CONCESSION, AND STARTING FIRES PRETTY MUCH EVERY-WHERE AT THE SAME TIME.
FIREWATCHERS BE DANGED!
THE WHOLE THING IS GONNA GET LIT UP REAL GOOD IN NO TIME. WE'RE GONNA LET HER RIP!! WE GONNA LET HER...

"...BURN!!!"

CAN'T YOU JUST SEE IT? ALL THOSE FOLKS OUT THERE RIGHT NOW, LINING UP TO SEE THE LIGHT SHOW? THEY'RE IN FOR QUITE A SPECTACLE TONIGHT, YES SIR!

BUT DON'T YOU WORRY, MIO AMICO, YOU WON'T HAVE TO WAIT FOR LONG. THE FIRE SHOULD COME DOWN THE PIKE SOON ENOUGH.

THE FIREMEN WILL STOP YOU! THEY'LL STOP THE FIRE!!

OH, YEAH? WITH WHAT WATER? WE ALREADY TOOK THE LIBERTY OF SHUTTING OFF THE WATER SUPPLY COMING FROM ARROWHEAD LAKE AND FROM THE CITY. AND WITHOUT WATER, NOT EVEN HALE'S BOYS WILL BE ABLE TO REIGN IN THE INFERNO.

AND THE JEFF GUARDS WILL BE SO BUSY TRYING TO SALVAGE THE VALUABLES FROM THE BUILDINGS THEY WON'T EVEN KNOW WHERE TO TURN WHEN THIS WHOLE PLACE COMES A'LIT.

DON'T ACT ALL SURPRISED! YOU ALREADY KNEW ABOUT THIS! YOU WERE RIGHT THERE WHEN WE SAID WE WERE GONNA MAKE THE FAIR HISTORY, REMEMBER?

WHY ARE YOU DOING THIS? WHY DO YOU HATE OUR FAIR SO MUCH?

HEY, IT AIN'T PERSONAL, KID -- JUST BUSINESS.

WE'VE GOT FINANCIAL INTERESTS TO PROTECT BACK HOME, CAPISCI? 'SIDES, YOU DIDN'T THINK THE POWERS THAT BE IN CHICAGO WOULD STOMACH BEING UPSTAGED BY ST. LOUIE, DID YA?

IT'S A SHAME YOU'RE GONNA MISS THE SHOW, BUT AT LEAST YOU'LL BE IN GOOD COMPANY. HA!

Grrrrr...

"HEY, DON'T WORRY, KID..."

"WE'RE JUST DOIN' OUR SHARE TO MAKE THIS EXPOSITION A TRULY MEMORABLE EVENT."

ROARRRR!

CHAPTER 3
END

1904

STORY
MARCELO VITAL

ART
DAVID MONTGOMERY

No single visit to the Louisiana Purchase Exposition is complete without a thrill. Every exhibit and every show always have something new to reveal, a new lesson to teach us. And don't be surprised if, at any given moment, you find yourself going from mere spectator to active participant.

The Fair has a way of pulling you into the action.

CHAPTER FOUR — *Illuminations*

Take Hagenbeck's Animal Paradise on the Pike for instance.

I've been there dozens of times to watch the show and all the wild animals they have there: tigers, bears, giant tortoises, sea-lions... even man-eating lions.

Only whenever I came to Hagenbeck's before, I was always on the other side of the bars.

WHACK!

DOWN, BRUTUS!!

I DON'T KNOW HOW YOU GOT IN HERE, BOY, BUT YOU BETTER GET OUT FAST, BEFORE MR. HAGENBECK CATCHES YA.

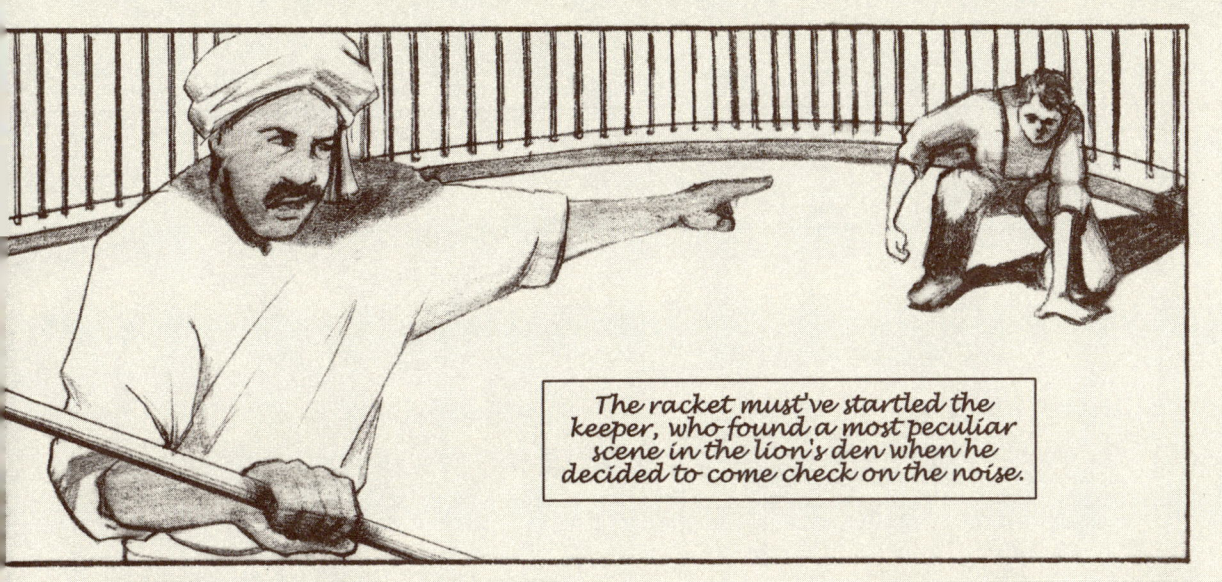

The racket must've startled the keeper, who found a most peculiar scene in the lion's den when he decided to come check on the noise.

"EASY, BOY!"

I would have stayed and explained myself...

...but there was no time to spare.

"NOW, DON'T YOU BE ORNERY, BRUTUS..."

HAGENBECK'S

Everyone at the Fair was in danger, and somebody had to do something!

If those thugs had their way, the Fair would go all to pieces as soon as the sun set and the lights came on.

That's when they were planning to cause an "accidental" power surge to explode electric transformers everywhere, turning the Fair into a bonfire bigger than Chicago in 1871.

And if there was one place where an "accident" like that could happen, it had to be at the Fair's power plant, in the Palace of Machinery.

I had to get there before sunset...

...no matter what got in my way.

Man alive!!

'SCUSE ME...

The fate of the Fair at stake, and I got caught in the jolly throng of humanity of the Pike!

And for once, I hadn't planned on it.

I should have remembered -- there's always a jolly throng on the Pike...

...day and night.

But soon I noticed this wasn't just another barker gathering a crowd for a new little thrill around the corner.

No, sir, this was big.

I had landed smack-dab in the middle of the Mysterious Asia Parade!

One of the largest attractions on the Pike, the parade is a procession of hundreds of gaily-costumed natives of the orient, each festooned with fabulous frocks from their homelands. They are a charming picture of eastern life -- a perfect Babel of odd-sounding languages and music strange to the ears.

PERSIA

> Entertaining the crowds are all manner of bizarre and exotic sights: Street musicians from Cairo, Persian dancers, Albanian gypsies, Cingalese devil dancers, Hindu acrobats, belly dancers and snake charmers, even an Egyptian juggler and fakir. Not to mention the endless procession of horses, donkeys, camels and dromedaries.

> At least, now I can say I've seen the elephant.

The whole pageant is quite the sight to behold and, under other circumstances, I'd have stayed to watch it. But not that day!

I needed to find a way outta there fast, and yelling fire in the middle of that crowd would just cause a stampede.

It was plain to see that going on foot wouldn't get me very far.

Thank goodness for the abundance of means of transportation that the World's Fair has to offer!

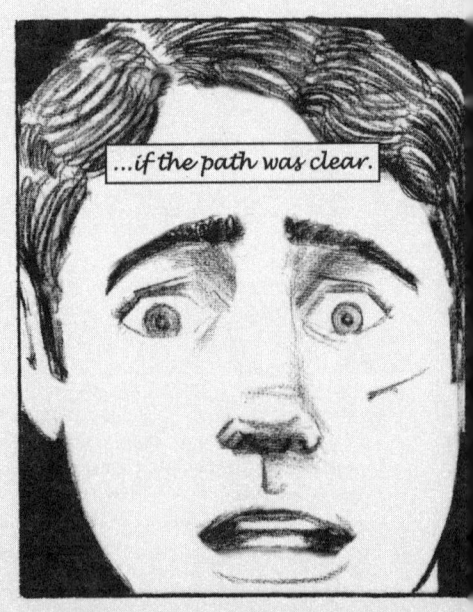

Not exactly Roosevelt's Rough Riders material, but I wasn't about to look this one in the mouth!

The power plant wasn't too far off. I'd be there in no time...

...if the path was clear.

Juliana de Kohl was the famous Holstein cow who came to the Fair all the way from California in her own individual train car, with two attendants to supply her every want. There had even been a crowd at the station waiting to welcome her.

A prized champion milk producer and a ballyhooed celebrity, Juliana was visiting the Fair in grand style.

I meant no disrespect, but right at that moment...

... Miss de Kohl was just another block in my road.

I'm sure if she knew the reason for my hurry, she'd forgive me my lack of manners.

CLOPT!

The sun was sinking fast in the horizon, and my heart was racing even faster.

Thousand of folks had begun to gather all around the Main Picture to watch the lights and fireworks...

...Claire among them.

If only they knew what they were really lining up for...

The Palace of Machinery is the World's Fair's powerhouse, containing the third largest power plant in the whole country.

Until a couple years ago, we didn't even know about electricity and suddenly we can't seem to live without it. Funny how fast we're getting so used to something so dangerously unpredictable.

But there was no time for my musings. I was there, but getting in wasn't going to be as easy as I thought. The big guy was guarding the entrance, disguised as a Jefferson Guard.

Altogether, the giant engines inside generate 45,000 horsepower, almost four times as much as Chicago's Columbian Exposition of 1893. The electrical power is created by state-of-the-art steam turbines and carried to all parts of the Fair for lighting, pumping, operating concessions and powering all kinds of new inventions.

It looked like I wouldn't be using the front door.

Fortunately, there're other ways to get into a Palace...

...including some that only a delivery boy would know about.

Getting up wasn't that hard. Getting down was a different story.

I saw them before I could figure out a way to the ground.

As I watched them approaching the main engines, I realized to my horror that they weren't alone in the Palace.

Thomas Edison himself, apparently inspecting the electrical systems he had helped install, was in there too!

THUNK

A most ill-timed inspection, I'm sure he'd agree.

I couldn't believe my eyes! They'd knocked Mr. Edison out cold!!

It was clear those ruffians would stop at nothing to accomplish their mission.

CrrrrrrrK...

But there was one thing I bet they weren't expecting.

So much for being stealthy.
PORCA MISERIA!
UGH!
THUD!
YOU WANNA PLAY HERO, RAGAZZO?
LET'S PLAY THEN...

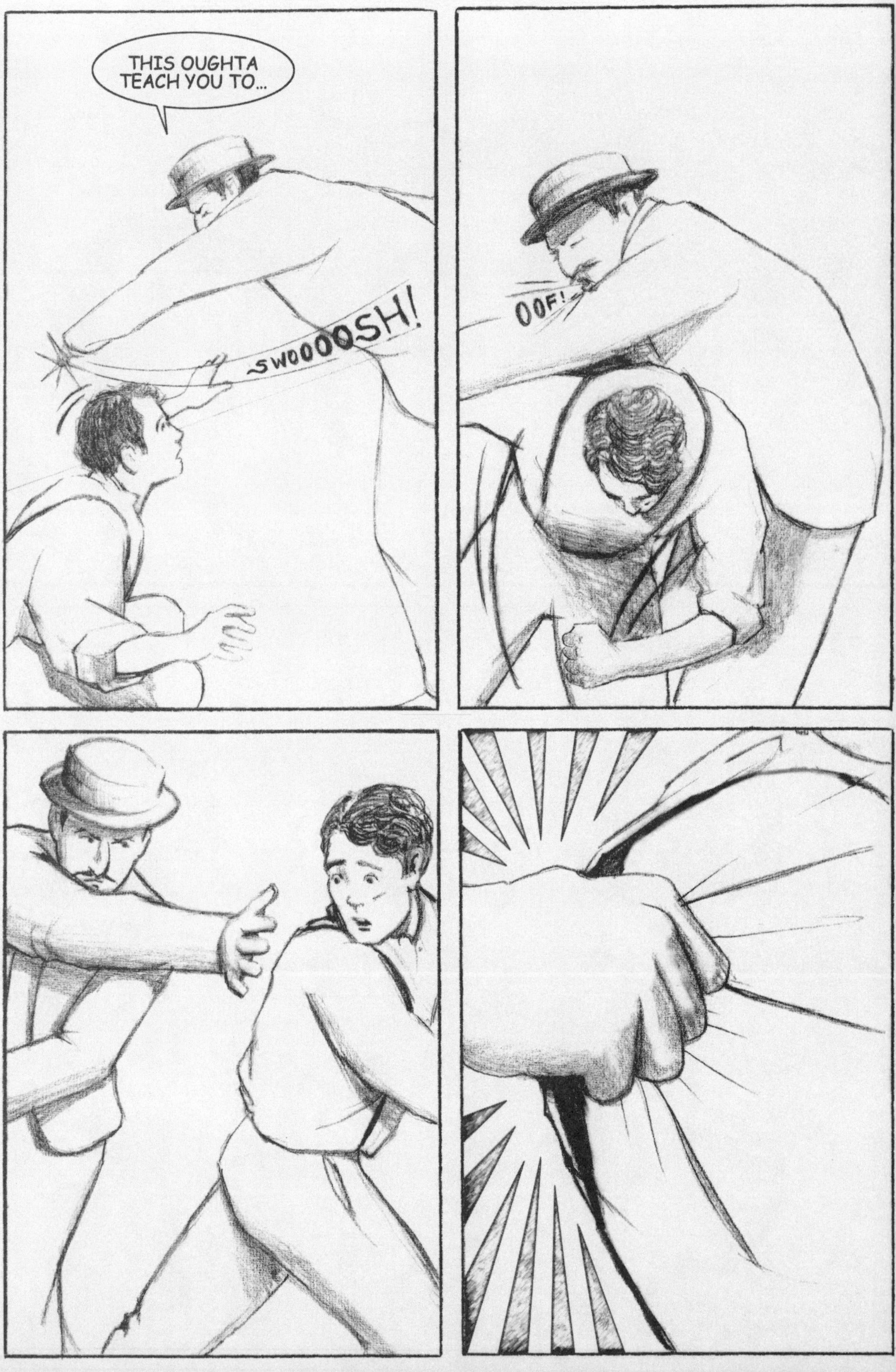
THIS OUGHTA TEACH YOU TO...
SWOOOOSH!
OOF!

NOWHERE TO RUN NOW, LITTLE FELLA -- THIS IS THE END. NO MORE NOSING AROUND FOR YOU.
ARRIVEDERCI, BAMBINO!!
CLUNK!
ZZZZZZ!

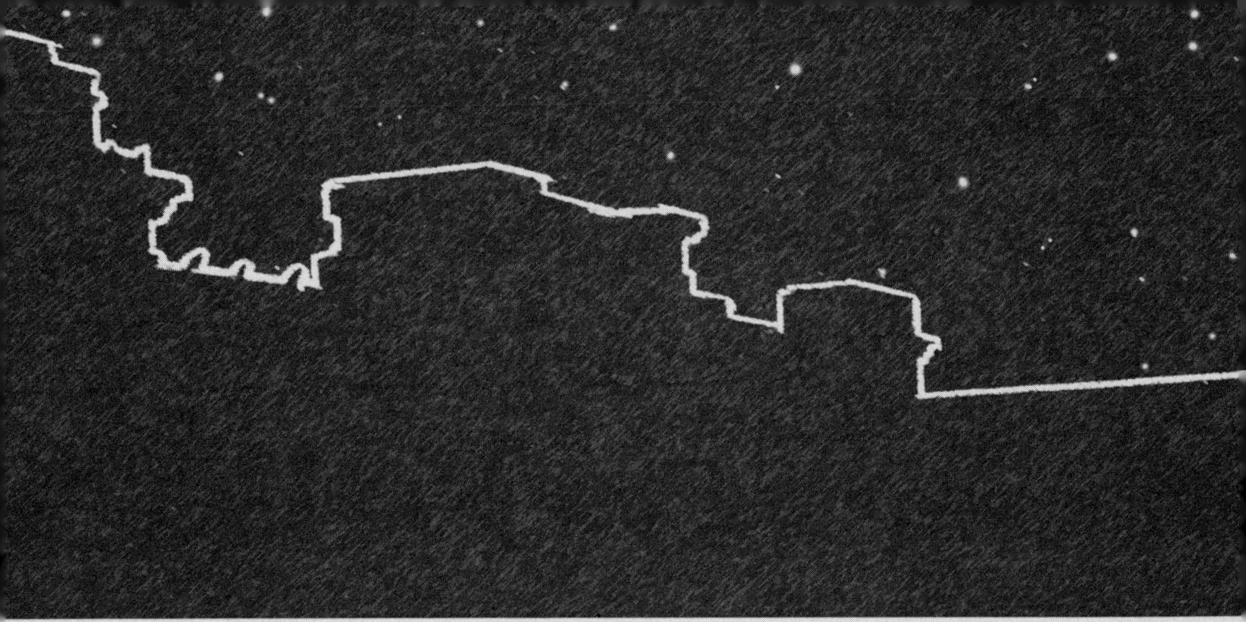

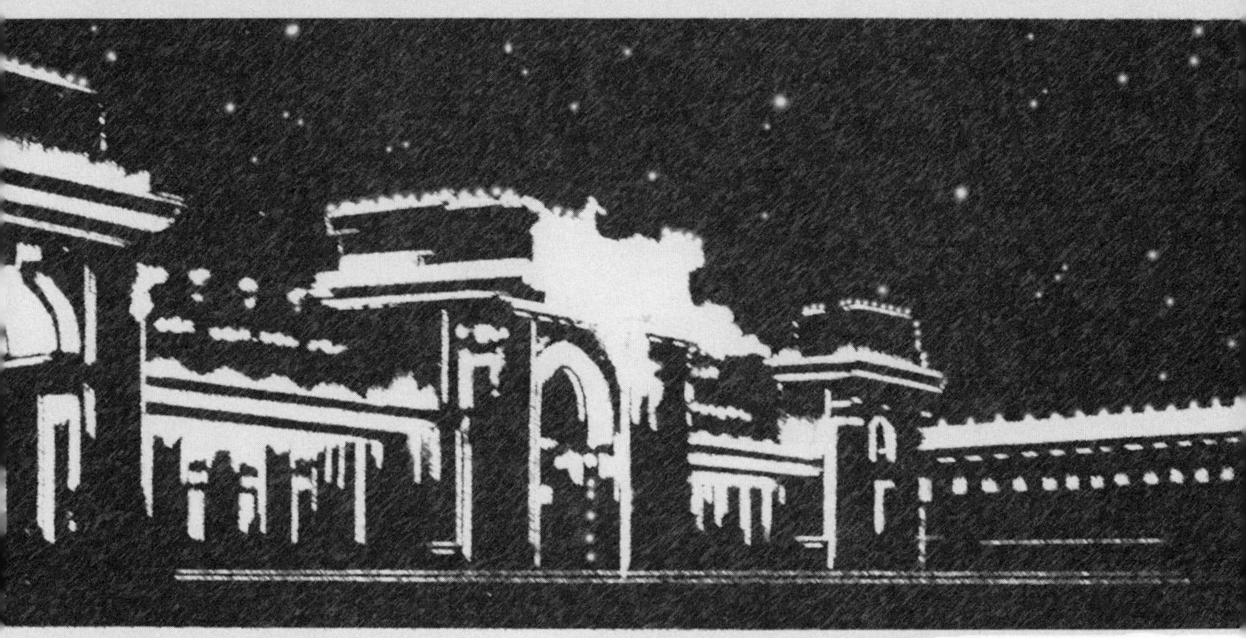

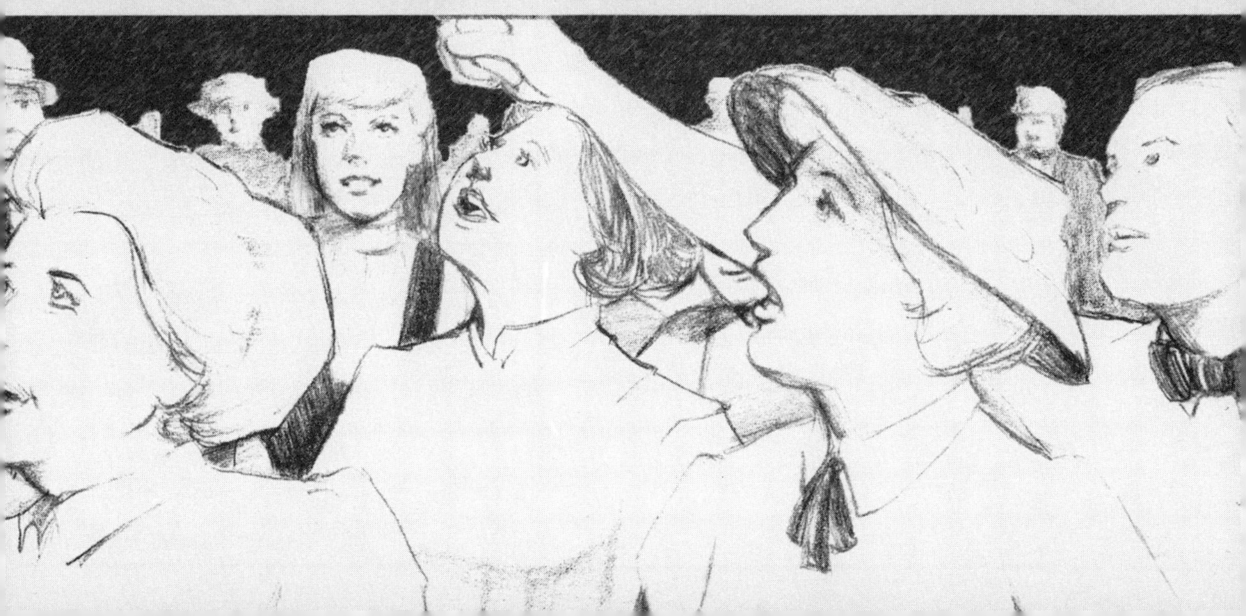

HEY, DANNY! JACK!!
WHAT HAPPENED HERE?
WHOAH!
JACK, WAKE UP! SVEGLIA! THE LIGHTS ARE ON, THERE'S NO FIRE AND DANNY... WELL, SOMETHING AIN'T RIGHT WITH DANNY.
SLAP SLAP
HUH?
MALEDIZIONE!! THAT STINKIN' LOMBARDO BOY!
LET'S SPLIT BEFORE HE GETS THE GUARDS HERE AND WE GET PINCHED.
GEE, WHAT ARE WE GONNA DO NOW? GO BACK TO CHICAGO?
ARE YOU CRAZY? THE BOSS'D HAVE US FOR LUNCH AFTER THIS FIASCO!
WE'RE GONNA HAFTA LAY LOW 'TIL THIS BLOWS OVER, CATCH THE FIRST TRAIN OUTTA HERE... DISAPPEAR FOR A WHILE.
I HEAR EVERYTHING IS UP-TO-DATE IN KANSAS CITY THESE DAYS. ANDIAMO!
OUCH...
WHAT HAPPENED, SON?
UH, MR. EDISON... I DON'T THINK YOU'D BELIEVE ME IF I TOLD YA.

So Mr. Edison thinks he was knocked unconscious by some mischievous kid that fell from the roof right on top of his head. And that's just as well, I reckon.

It'd only cause a frenzy of scared folks to flee the fairgrounds in hysterics and spoil the Fair for a lot of people.

Yep, I'd probably get more medals than Owney, the traveling mail dog, if I told the police all that had happened that day, but what good would it do?

Those thugs would have won in the end.

No, that's not how I wanted my Fair to end.

A place like this deserves a grand finale fit for its majesty.

And there's nothing grander than seeing the Fair at night, transformed into a fairyland of electric lights -- it's like the buildings themselves are made of light, shining brighter than the stars above.

The thousands of colored light bulbs perfectly reflected in the waters of the Grand Basin made for the most beautiful thing I have ever seen in all my born days.

Well, the second most beautiful.

It's almost too sad to think that the Fair will end soon, that all this will be gone before long. The gates will close, the lights will be turned off and the buildings will be torn down. The Ferris Wheel will be dismantled, the Palaces will crumble and the Pike will cease to exist, except in our memories.

But at least those memories will never fade away.

> The Fair gave us a new measure of all that we can be, all that we can become in our lives. It showed us the world in ways we have never seen before, made us look back into our history and forward into the future.

> And what a future it'll be! If now we can talk to other cities through a wire, imagine what we'll be able to do in a hundred years! The Louisiana Purchase Exposition taught us that there are no limits to what we can do, no end to what we can create.

In a hundred years, will the world be a better place? I don't know. All I know is that the 1904 World's Fair gave us reason to do better, to strive for more. Like Mr. Francis said, it gave us inspiration for even greater achievements.

If we take that lesson to heart, the Fair's legacy will live on forever.

MOM? I THINK I FOUND WHAT I WAS LOOKING FOR.

THE END

"Trust thyself; every heart vibrates to that iron string. Accept the place divine providence has found for you, the society of your contemporaries, the connection of events."

- David R. Francis quoting Ralph Waldo Emerson -

Dedicated to the people of St. Louis, past and present. To those who made the 1904 World's Fair possible and to those who keep its legacy alive.

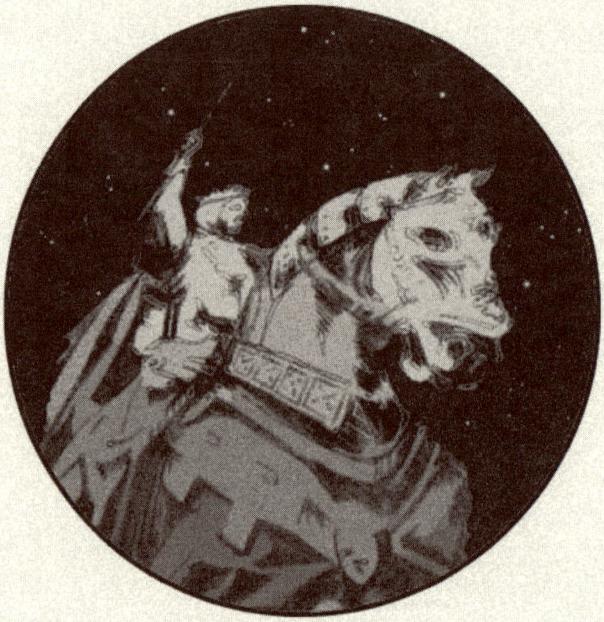

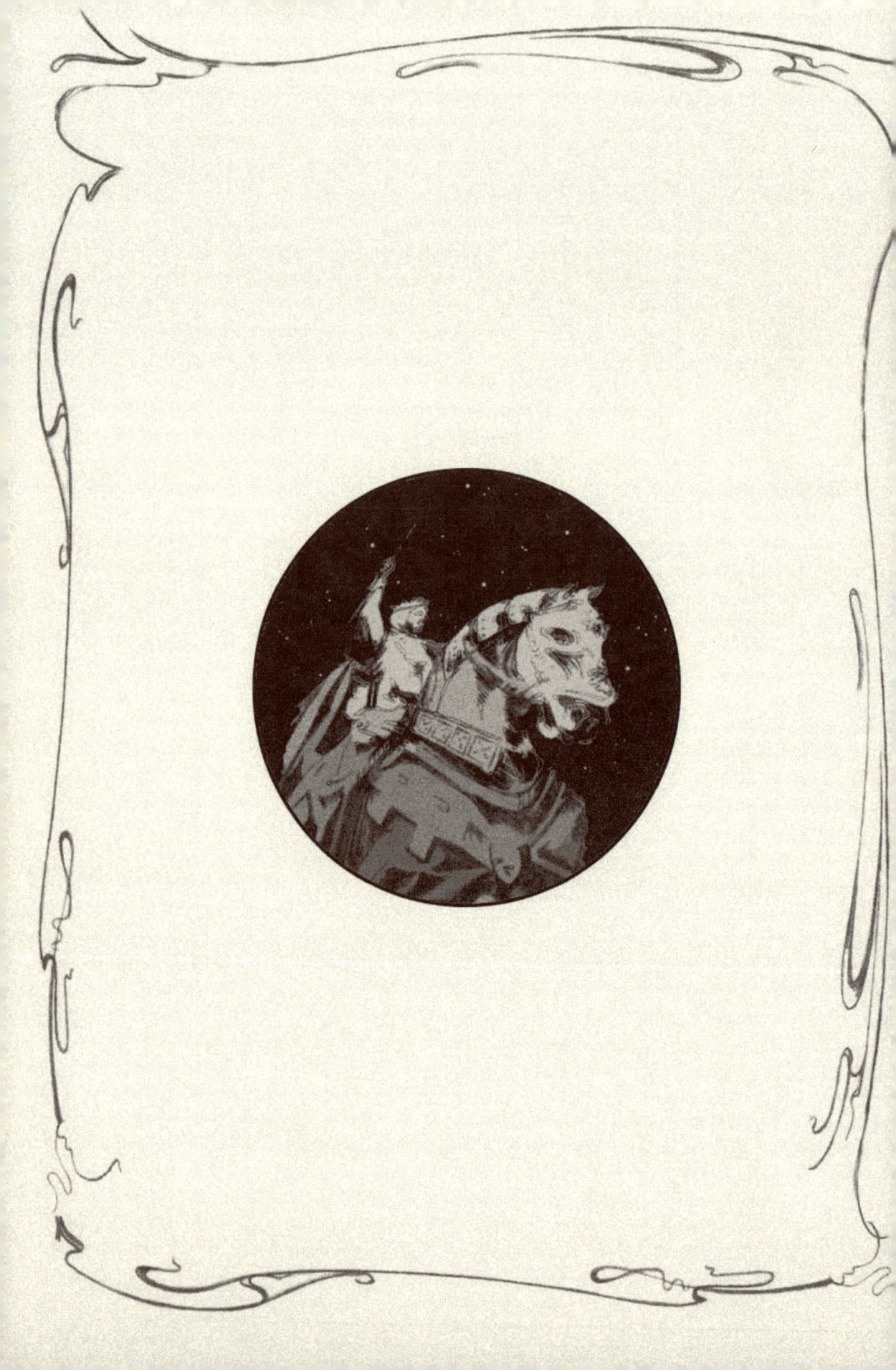

1904

STORY
MARCELO VITAL
ART
DAVID MONTGOMERY

Further Readings

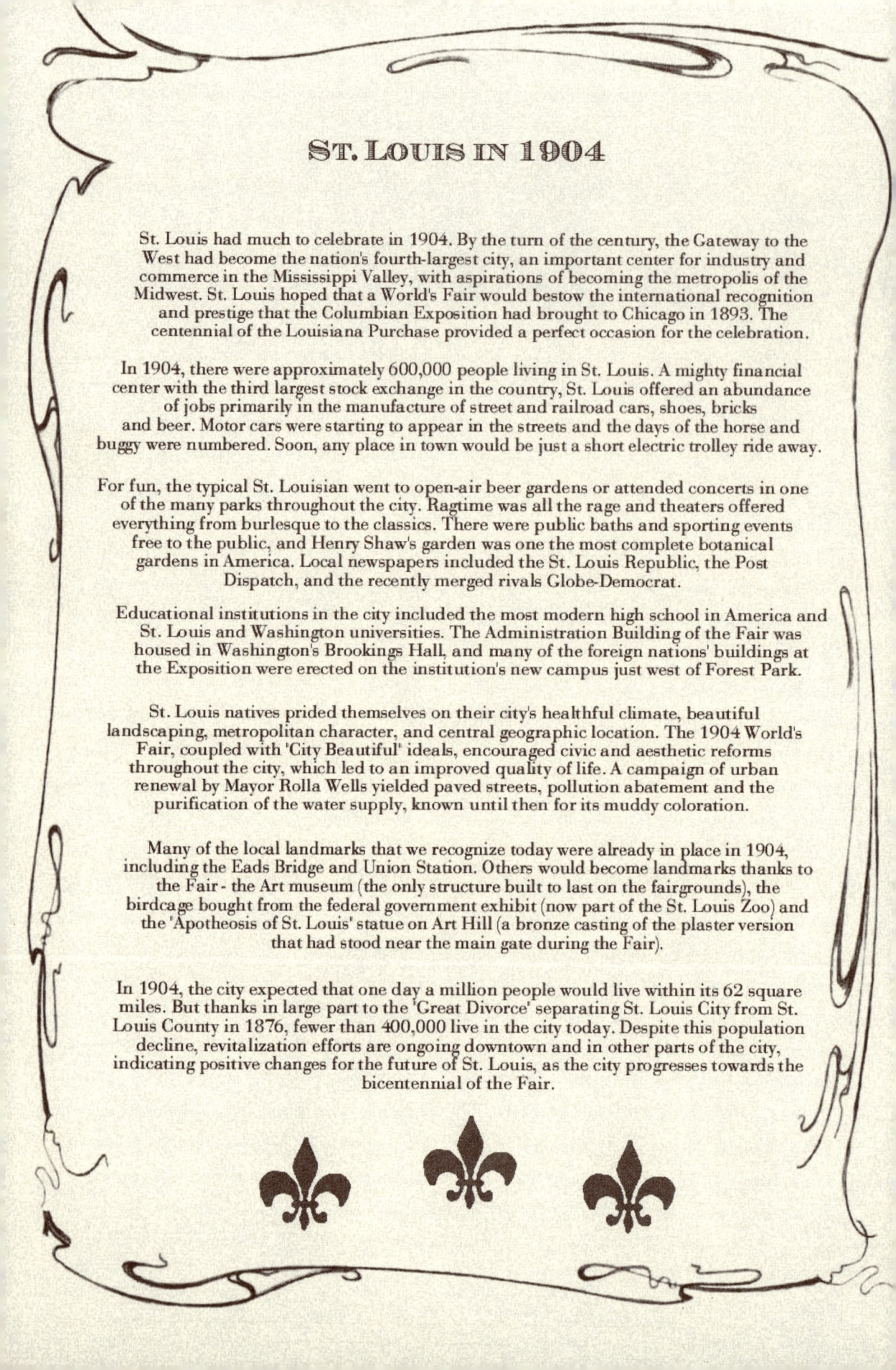

St. Louis in 1904

St. Louis had much to celebrate in 1904. By the turn of the century, the Gateway to the West had become the nation's fourth-largest city, an important center for industry and commerce in the Mississippi Valley, with aspirations of becoming the metropolis of the Midwest. St. Louis hoped that a World's Fair would bestow the international recognition and prestige that the Columbian Exposition had brought to Chicago in 1893. The centennial of the Louisiana Purchase provided a perfect occasion for the celebration.

In 1904, there were approximately 600,000 people living in St. Louis. A mighty financial center with the third largest stock exchange in the country, St. Louis offered an abundance of jobs primarily in the manufacture of street and railroad cars, shoes, bricks and beer. Motor cars were starting to appear in the streets and the days of the horse and buggy were numbered. Soon, any place in town would be just a short electric trolley ride away.

For fun, the typical St. Louisian went to open-air beer gardens or attended concerts in one of the many parks throughout the city. Ragtime was all the rage and theaters offered everything from burlesque to the classics. There were public baths and sporting events free to the public, and Henry Shaw's garden was one the most complete botanical gardens in America. Local newspapers included the St. Louis Republic, the Post Dispatch, and the recently merged rivals Globe-Democrat.

Educational institutions in the city included the most modern high school in America and St. Louis and Washington universities. The Administration Building of the Fair was housed in Washington's Brookings Hall, and many of the foreign nations' buildings at the Exposition were erected on the institution's new campus just west of Forest Park.

St. Louis natives prided themselves on their city's healthful climate, beautiful landscaping, metropolitan character, and central geographic location. The 1904 World's Fair, coupled with 'City Beautiful' ideals, encouraged civic and aesthetic reforms throughout the city, which led to an improved quality of life. A campaign of urban renewal by Mayor Rolla Wells yielded paved streets, pollution abatement and the purification of the water supply, known until then for its muddy coloration.

Many of the local landmarks that we recognize today were already in place in 1904, including the Eads Bridge and Union Station. Others would become landmarks thanks to the Fair - the Art museum (the only structure built to last on the fairgrounds), the birdcage bought from the federal government exhibit (now part of the St. Louis Zoo) and the 'Apotheosis of St. Louis' statue on Art Hill (a bronze casting of the plaster version that had stood near the main gate during the Fair).

In 1904, the city expected that one day a million people would live within its 62 square miles. But thanks in large part to the 'Great Divorce' separating St. Louis City from St. Louis County in 1876, fewer than 400,000 live in the city today. Despite this population decline, revitalization efforts are ongoing downtown and in other parts of the city, indicating positive changes for the future of St. Louis, as the city progresses towards the bicentennial of the Fair.

The Italian Hill in 1904

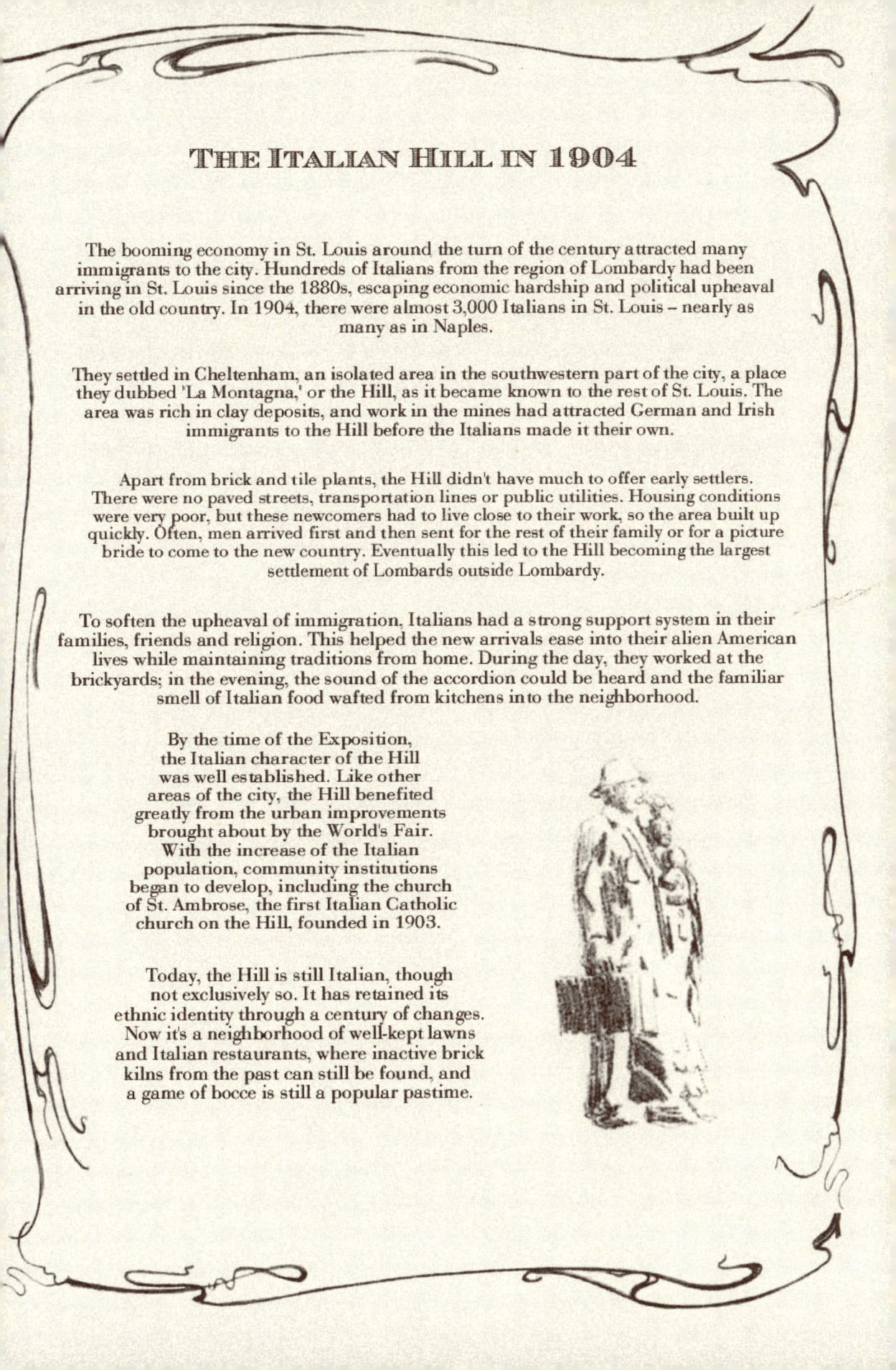

The booming economy in St. Louis around the turn of the century attracted many immigrants to the city. Hundreds of Italians from the region of Lombardy had been arriving in St. Louis since the 1880s, escaping economic hardship and political upheaval in the old country. In 1904, there were almost 3,000 Italians in St. Louis – nearly as many as in Naples.

They settled in Cheltenham, an isolated area in the southwestern part of the city, a place they dubbed 'La Montagna,' or the Hill, as it became known to the rest of St. Louis. The area was rich in clay deposits, and work in the mines had attracted German and Irish immigrants to the Hill before the Italians made it their own.

Apart from brick and tile plants, the Hill didn't have much to offer early settlers. There were no paved streets, transportation lines or public utilities. Housing conditions were very poor, but these newcomers had to live close to their work, so the area built up quickly. Often, men arrived first and then sent for the rest of their family or for a picture bride to come to the new country. Eventually this led to the Hill becoming the largest settlement of Lombards outside Lombardy.

To soften the upheaval of immigration, Italians had a strong support system in their families, friends and religion. This helped the new arrivals ease into their alien American lives while maintaining traditions from home. During the day, they worked at the brickyards; in the evening, the sound of the accordion could be heard and the familiar smell of Italian food wafted from kitchens into the neighborhood.

By the time of the Exposition, the Italian character of the Hill was well established. Like other areas of the city, the Hill benefited greatly from the urban improvements brought about by the World's Fair. With the increase of the Italian population, community institutions began to develop, including the church of St. Ambrose, the first Italian Catholic church on the Hill, founded in 1903.

Today, the Hill is still Italian, though not exclusively so. It has retained its ethnic identity through a century of changes. Now it's a neighborhood of well-kept lawns and Italian restaurants, where inactive brick kilns from the past can still be found, and a game of bocce is still a popular pastime.

The 1904 Olympic Games

The Louisiana Purchase Exposition wasn't the only notable event taking place in St. Louis in 1904. The city was also hosting the first ever Olympic Games in the United States. The Games, revived in 1896 in Athens and staged in Paris in 1900, were to be held in Chicago in 1904. But when Fair president David Francis announced that a large physical culture exhibition would take place at the Fair, the Olympic Committee, fearing poor attendance in the Windy City, granted the Olympics to St. Louis.

The Olympic Games were held at Washington University's brand new campus featuring a state-of-the-art gymnasium, track and field, and a modern stadium - the first in the world built of concrete. Francis Field and Francis Gymnasium, honoring the Fair's president, are still in use today. Swimming events took place at the Life-Saving Exhibit lake at the Fair, a less-than-adequate venue. In addition to the more traditional competitions, the 1904 games also included more unorthodox events like bowling on the green, tug-of-war and roque (a form of croquet).

For the United States, it was a smashing victory, as the vast majority of athletes were Americans. Taking part in the games was not an easy task for international competitors, who had to pay for their own trip. Since only a few countries sent representatives, and often American athletic groups competed against each other, most medals went to the U.S.

The games themselves were a far cry from the Olympic Games we know today. One of the most peculiar events was the marathon: A runner hitched a ride in a motorcar to win the gold medal, but lost it moments later to the real winner, who crossed the finish line at death's door, carried by a concoction of raw eggs, strychnine and brandy. Native peoples from the Anthropological Exhibit participated on special days at the Olympic Games, with some events even pitting Patagonians against Pygmies.

In truth, the Games served as just one more attraction of the Louisiana Purchase Exposition. In the end, there were more organ concerts at the Fair than Olympic events. But what those early games lacked in organization was compensated for by the commitment of the participants and the response of those in the bleachers. The Olympic Games were yet another laurel on St. Louis' crown in 1904.

MEET ME IN ST. LOUIS

Even though 'moving pictures' were exhibited at the Fair, movie-making was at its infancy at the turn of the century. But forty years later, the 1904 World's Fair would be the heart of one of the America's most beloved motion picture musicals.

Meet Me in St. Louis features the Fair itself only in its final minutes, but the Exposition's very existence is the driving force behind the story. The movie was based on '5135 Kensington Avenue,' a book of short stories by St. Louis native Sally Smith Benson about her childhood memories. It depicts a year in the life of the Smiths, a typical St. Louis family, shaken by the prospect of missing the Fair when Mr. Smith announces his decision to move the family to New York. His four daughters, his wife, grandpa and housekeeper are devastated. Of course, this being a musical, the family gets a happy Hollywood ending and attends Illuminations at the Fair.

The movie ushered in a golden age of musicals for MGM and established Vincent Minnelli as one of the best directors of the day. It was his first feature in Technicolor and the one in which he met his future bride, Judy Garland. Garland played the role of Esther, one of the Smith daughters, a part she was reluctant to play at first, but that became one of the highlights of her career. The other star of the movie is seven-year-old Margaret O'Brien, who played Esther's little sister Tootie. She received a mini-Oscar statuette for her role.

Meet Me in St. Louis was one of the first movies to combine music and storyline to further the tale and not only to showcase the singing and dancing talents of its stars. Many musical sequences would become classics, and some already were. The title song had been the most popular tune in St. Louis in 1904. New compositions, such as "The Trolley Song" and "Have Yourself a Merry Little Christmas," would become Garland standards. Alas, the only musical number taking place at the Fair ended up on the cutting room floor: Rogers and Hammerstein's "Boys and Girls like You and Me" didn't quite fit the mood of the finale.

When *Meet Me in St. Louis* Opened in 1944, America was at war and the public was thirsting for lighter, more optimistic fare. Hollywood was looking back at happier, more peaceful times and the utopian world of the Fair inspired Minelli to create a masterpiece, where troubles were miles away and the future still seemed bright.

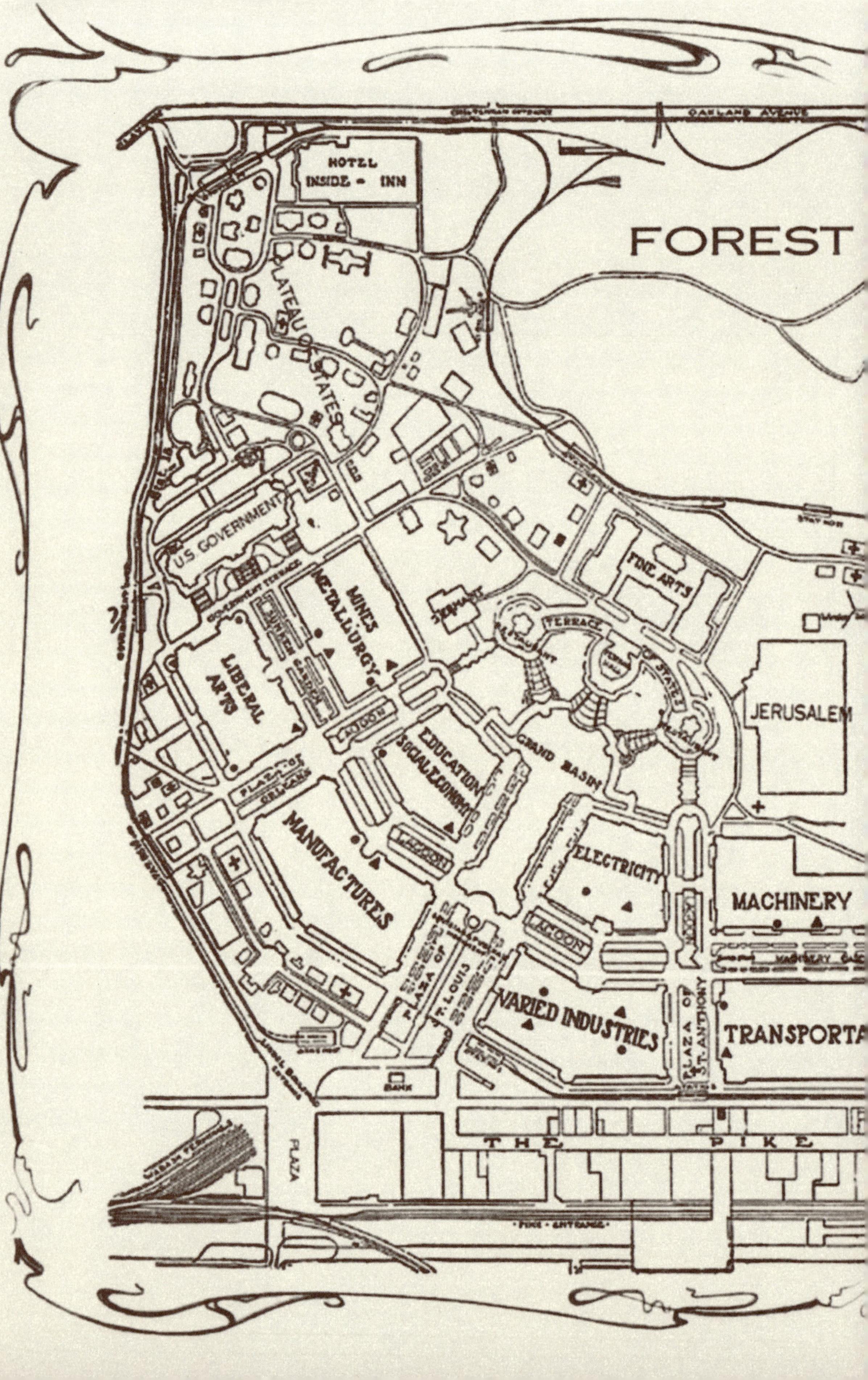

OAKLAND AVENUE
HOTEL INSIDE - INN
FOREST
PLATEAU OF STATES
U.S. GOVERNMENT
FINE ARTS
MINES METALLURGY
LIBERAL ARTS
TERRACE OF STATES
JERUSALEM
GRAND BASIN
EDUCATION SOCIAL ECONOMY
PLAZA OF ORLEANS
LAGOON
MANUFACTURES
ELECTRICITY
MACHINERY
PLAZA OF ST. LOUIS
VARIED INDUSTRIES
PLAZA OF ST. ANTHONY
TRANSPORTA
BANK
THE PIKE
PLAZA
PIKE ENTRANCE

Lousiana Purchase Exposition

Forest Park
St. Louis
Missouri

1904

For more information and to access
The 1904 Companion, please visit
www.1904ishere.com